THE STORY
OF FUZZYPEG
THE HEDGEHOG

BASED ON THE STORIES BY

Alison Uttley and *Margaret Tempest*

An imprint of HarperCollins*Publishers*

The Story of Fuzzypeg the Hedgehog
was first published in 1932 by William Heinemann Ltd
This edition was first published in Great Britain by HarperCollins*Publishers* Ltd in 2000
Published by arrangement with Egmont Children's Books Ltd

1 3 5 7 9 10 8 6 4 2
ISBN: 0-00-710012-4

Text for this edition by Susan Dickinson based on the
television adaptation by Helen Cresswell
Text © The Alison Uttley Literary Property Trust 2000
Illustrations in this work derived from the television series © HTV LTD 2000
based on the original illustrations by Margaret Tempest.
Production of the television series by United Productions in association with Cosgrove Hall

The HarperCollins website address is: www.**fire**and**water**.com

Printed and bound in Hong Kong

ONE MORNING Milkman Hedgehog got up specially early. He walked up little Grey Rabbit's path with his milk pails.

"You're early this morning, Hedgehog," she said to him when she opened the door.

"Yes, Grey Rabbit. It's my little Fuzzypeg's birthday."

"How old is he?"

"A whole year! Half growed up!"

"Wait a moment, I'll send him a present." And little Grey Rabbit disappeared back into the house.

Very soon little Grey
Rabbit came back. She
was holding an egg.

"It's a hard-boiled
egg. I boiled it all day.
Little Fuzzypeg can play
ball with it."

"Why, thank you kindly, Grey Rabbit," said Hedgehog.

Hedgehog had many calls to make before he went
home for his breakfast. And he told everyone he met
that it was Fuzzypeg's
birthday.

Moldy Warp gave
him a scrambled egg
he had scrambled
under a haystack
to find.

Rat gave him a poached egg he had poached from the farm the night before and the Red Squirrel gave him an old-laid egg.

When Hedgehog got home he gave all the eggs to Fuzzypeg.

"I like Grey Rabbit's best," said Fuzzypeg. "Can I play ball with it later?"

"Of course you can," said his father, smiling kindly.

Later that morning, Hedgehog said, "Come on, son. You and me will go and have a good game of rolling."

So Fuzzypeg and his father went to the hill, curled themselves into balls and rolled and rolled down it.

Halfway down, the Red Squirrel's egg broke! What a horrible smell!

"That Red Squirrel! I've a good mind to give him no milk. Giving you a rotten egg!" said Hedgehog. So they found another hill, and rolled and rolled all day.

And then it was time
to go home and for
Fuzzypeg to get his
present.

When he opened it he
found a small white cage.
Inside were two little black insects with glowing tails.

"Ooh, what are they?" he gasped.

"Glow-worms. Two tame glow-worms," said Hedgehog.
And when Fuzzypeg went to bed he hung the cage from
a hook and fell asleep with the room glowing with light.

One fine day, soon afterwards, Fuzzypeg and his father were strolling through the fields near the farm. Suddenly they heard a great cackling…

"Help! Help! Save us!" cried the hens, running and squawking towards them.

"Oh! Oh!" cried Fuzzypeg, when he saw the adder chasing them. "Let's run, Father!"

But Hedgehog let go of Fuzzypeg's hand and sprang at the adder. He seized its tail and held on tight.

The adder twisted and turned, and tried to bite Hedgehog, but it only got a mouthful of prickles. At last, it lay still.

"Come on, son. Hadder pie for supper tonight," said Hedgehog and he slung the adder over his shoulder.

"Oh, Father, you *are* brave," said Fuzzypeg.

"Three cheers for Hedgehog!" cried everyone.

On their way home Fuzzypeg spied his cousins Tim and
Bill Hedgehog.

"I say, you fellows! My father killed a hadder!" he
cried. "He pounced on it, yes, he pounced on it and
held the tip-tippet of its tail till it was dead!"

"That's nothing," said Tim. "My father pounced on a
lion's tail and held it till it was dead!"

"Oh," said Fuzzypeg.

When the Hedgehog family were at supper, eating
their hadder pie, Fuzzypeg turned to his mother.

"Mother," he asked. "If my father met a lion, could he pounce on its tail and hold tight till it was dead?"

"Of course he could," his mother replied.

"I'm going to be brave, I'm going to be very, very brave, like Father!" said Fuzzypeg.

"Well, you can start by going tomorrow, all by yourself, to see Speckledy Hen. I've made her some hayseed cake."

The next morning Mrs Hedgehog kissed Fuzzypeg goodbye. "Now mind you walk on the little green path and not on the broad white road across the fields. There are dangers about."

"What shall I do if I meet a danger, Mother?"

"Why, roll up in a ball and keep your face hidden."

Fuzzypeg took the hayseed cake to Speckledy Hen and she showed him where the finest acorns fall. He gathered some up in his hanky to take with him. Then he started for home. He hadn't gone far when he saw Hare, sitting on a grassy bank.

"Stop a minute, young Fuzzypeg!" called Hare. "Come and play noughts and crosses."

So Fuzzypeg sat down beside Hare and together they played

noughts and crosses. Suddenly Fuzzypeg noticed it was nearly dark. He jumped up, waved to Hare and set off.

He looked at the little green path by the hedge – but a stoat might jump out at him that way. He decided to take the broad white road across the field.

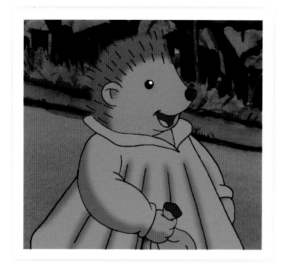

"My father's brave, and so am I," he sang to himself as he trudged along. "My father's brave, and so am I."

"Woof! Woof! Woof!"

"A lion! Help!" shrieked Fuzzypeg. He kicked off his red shoes and rolled himself into a tight little ball.

"Good dog!" said a voice. And a large hanky was dropped over Fuzzypeg. He was carried away, and soon afterwards put down on a path.

He tried to scamper off, but a big red flower pot was placed on top of him.

"You stop there and I'll bring you some food. Come on, Spot! Good boy." The footsteps went away and Fuzzypeg was all alone in the dark.

"You let me go!" he called. "My father's a great hedgehog and he once killed a lion!

"Oh, oh!" he sobbed, but nobody heard him.

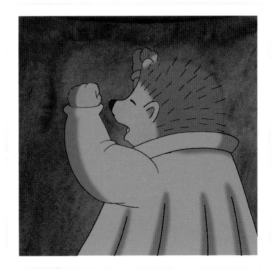

"Fuzzypeg! Fuzzypeg!" called
Hedgehog as he crossed the meadow
looking for his son. He found a piece
of paper with noughts and crosses
on it and a little further on he found
scattered acorns and a pair of little red shoes.

Hedgehog ran to Grey Rabbit's house and banged
on the door.

"Hedgehog, what are you doing here? No milk tonight,
thank you," said Squirrel, when she opened the door.

"Please, it's my little Fuzzypeg. He's lost."

"Has anyone seen
Fuzzypeg?" called
Squirrel.

"I have," shouted
Hare. "We met in the
Long Meadow and had
a game of noughts and
crosses. Yes, that's it,

the very paper!" he said, when Hedgehog showed him the paper he had found.

"Oh dear, I am so sorry Hedgehog," said little Grey Rabbit. "I think you should see Wise Owl."

So Hedgehog ran through the wood to Wise Owl's tree. He waved his hanky and Wise Owl looked out.

"To-whoo! What do you want?" hooted Wise Owl.

"Please sir, I've lost my Fuzzypeg and Grey Rabbit thought you could find him for me."

"Perhaps I can. But I must be paid."

"Anything you like."

"Well, I will have a quill for a pen, a can of milk and a new-laid egg. Bring them tomorrow at dawn, and you shall have news of your son." And Wise Owl soared up into the night sky.

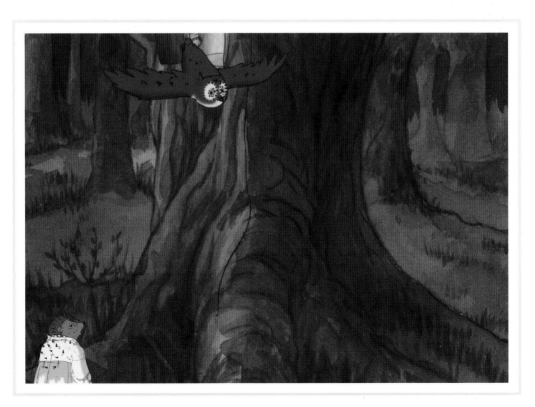

He flew over the fields and he circled over the farmyard.

Then Wise Owl flew over the farmer's garden where his sharp eyes spied an upside down flower pot.

Down he went and he heard a little voice:

"I'm trying to be brave. I'm trying. Mother, Father, come. Please come!"

Wise Owl landed on the edge of the pot.

"Is that you, little hedgehog?"

"Yes, yes, it's me, Fuzzypeg!"

"Help is coming! To-whoo!" And Wise Owl flew off.

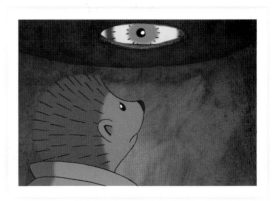

Early the next morning
Hedgehog walked up to
Wise Owl's house with
a can of milk, a new-
laid egg and a quill for
a pen. He rang the
little silver bell.

"Leave them there, Hedgehog," said Wise Owl.
"I have found your son. He is safe under a flower pot
in the farmer's garden."

Hedgehog thanked him and started home at a run,
calling on his way for little Grey Rabbit, Hare, Squirrel
and Moldy Warp. Then Mrs Hedgehog ran to join
them and they all set off through the fields until they
reached the farmer's garden.

They ran down the path, and there was the flower pot!

"Are you there, Fuzzypeg?" called Hedgehog.

"Ooh, yes, Father. Are you?"

"Oh, thank goodness!" said Mrs Hedgehog.

"All push, and over the flower pot must go," Hedgehog shouted to the others.

So they pushed and they pushed, but the plant pot didn't move.

"Now, all push together!" said Hedgehog.
"All together – shove!"

"Push harder! Push harder!" called
Fuzzypeg from inside the pot.

But still the pot did not move.

Then Moldy Warp came up.

He looked at them all and shook his
head. "Watch me," he said. "This is the way!"

And he began to dig.

The earth flew up in a shower and soon Moldy Warp
had disappeared. Mr and Mrs Hedgehog, little Grey
Rabbit, Squirrel and
Hare waited to see
what would happen
next.

Suddenly a tiny nose
appeared, and there
was Fuzzypeg!

"Hurray!" shouted Fuzzypeg.
"Hurray!" shouted the others.

Back they all went to the Hedgehogs' house for a celebration. There were acorns baked in their skins and fresh blackberries with cream. And when they went home they each took a small quill pen which Hedgehog had made for them.

But Moldy Warp said that digging was more in his line than writing and he had everything he wanted in his castle under the Ten Acre Field.